Charlie Cheetah and the Chain

The Apex of the Food Pyramid

Written by **Muhammad Wadee**

Inspired by a true story

Illustrated by **Shayle Bester**

AuthorHouse™ UK
1663 Liberty Drive
Bloomington, IN 47403 USA
www.authorhouse.co.uk
UK TFN: 0800 0148641 (Toll Free inside the UK)
UK Local: 02036 956322 (+44 20 3695 6322 from outside the UK)

Interior Image Credit: Shayle Bester

ISBN: 979-8-8230-8282-2 (sc)
979-8-8230-8281-5 (e)

Print information available on the last page.

Published by AuthorHouse 08/22/2023

Acknowledgments

I would like to thank my sisters Ammaarah, Taskeen and Mahdiyyah for inspiring me, and my late grandfather Dr Khalid Ismail who encouraged me to always have a thirst for knowledge, to discover by questioning and to have an enquiring mind. Thank you to my grandmother Khadija from Polokwane who has encouraged me to love reading, to explore science and to always be creative. Thank you to my paternal grandparents, Suliman and Julie, and my parents, Ashraf and Kareema, who have taken me on so many game driving adventures to the Kruger National Park. To see animals in their natural environment, has been my inspiration.

Special thanks to the Hoedspruit Endangered Species Centre (HESC) for inspiring me to get involved with animal conservation and for assisting me with photographs for my publication. Thank you to all those unnamed heroes and heroines out there who are selflessly involved in animal conservation. Together our conservation efforts can raise awareness on the importance of conserving ecosystems. We can make a difference to improve the survival of all living species in this one and only biosphere, called Earth, that we know.

Muhammad Wadee

For planet Earth

Foreword

My Heart Leaps Up

My heart leaps up when I behold
A rainbow in the sky:
So was it when my life began;
So is it now I am a man;
So be it when I shall grow old,
Or let me die!
The Child is father of the Man;
And I could wish my days to be
Bound each to each by natural piety.

William Wordsworth

Our magnificent universe is run by an important law that is often forgotten, the Law of Attraction.

Because of our connection with a universal energy, our positive thoughts and feelings have the ability to steer and bring this positive energy force back to us. Our thoughts have a frequency. Positive thoughts attract positive things. We should not be disheartened by the challenges that our Earth faces but we should look at it with a positive attitude, beginning by being grateful for the abundance that we already have on planet Earth.

Once we start to appreciate our planet and we start to live from a space of abundance and piety, we will realize ourselves, the importance of change. Every change matters.

Khadija Ismail

"Cherish the natural world, because you're a part of it and you depend on it."

Sir David Attenborough

I

t's a hot day on the African savannah and Little Charlie Cheetah is sitting in his den.

His mum always worries about him.

'Stay close, my little one," she whispers
as she leaves to hunt. 'Don't wander
away from the den. I wouldn't
want you to get lost in
these vast plains.'

4

Charlie watches her from a distance. He is in awe of her because when she hunts, she reaches speeds of 110 kilometers per hour.

Charlie is extremely proud to be a cheetah because cheetahs are the fastest mammals on land. Their bodies are adapted to reach these top speeds and they are able to change direction very quickly.

While watching his mum, Charlie sees impala everywhere. They are so thin that they look sick. This is because the land is overpopulated with impala and warthogs. The land is dry and the animals have eaten all the grass. Little Charlie ponders over the imbalance in the environment. It makes him sad.

As Little Charlie and mum dig their noses deep into their food later that day, mum explains that he is an apex predator. He likes being an apex predator.

'You play a big role in keeping the fine balance between the food chain and the ecosystem,' Mum explains.

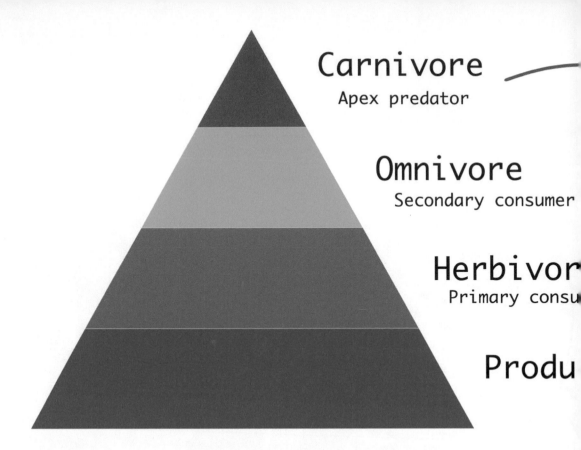

Carnivore
Apex predator

Omnivore
Secondary consumer

Herbivor
Primary consu

Produ

Charlie knows all about food chains and ecosystems. The organisms at the bottom of the food chain are the producers. Most producers are plants which make their own food from non-living sources of energy. The plants are so clever that they are able to capture the sun's energy. They then convert it into a form that they, and the animals that eat the producers, can use. Animals that eat producers are called consumers.

's

Primary consumers feed on plants to get the energy they need. They are not only called primary consumers, they are also called herbivores, which is a fancy name that describes an animal that eats plants. Ivan Impala is a primary consumer. Animals, like Collin the Caracal, are secondary consumers. They eat the primary consumers to get energy from them. Charlie is a tertiary consumer because he is a meat eater, or carnivore.

Primary, secondary and tertiary consumers work at different levels to make up what we call a food chain.

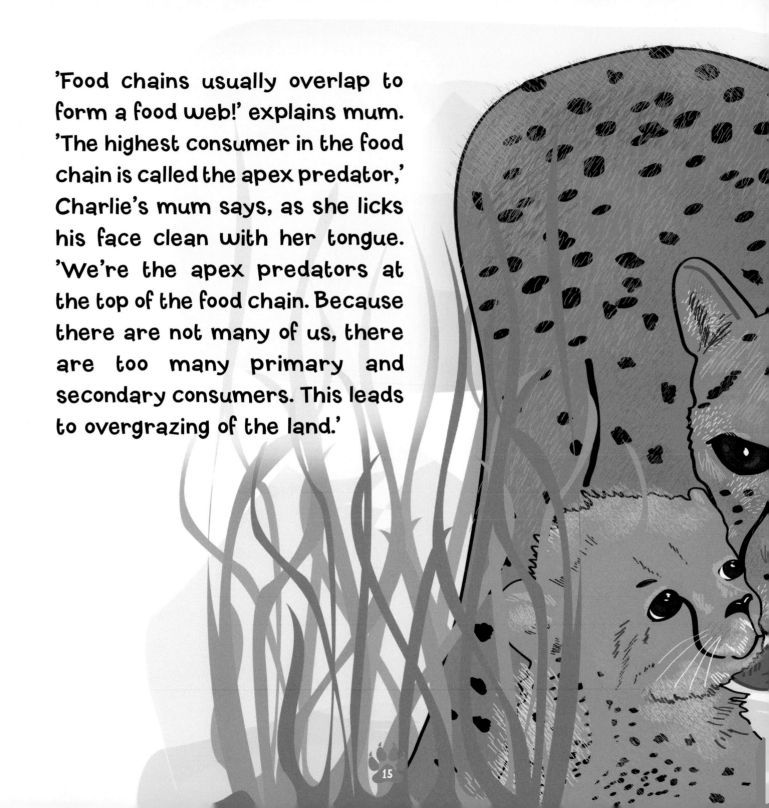

'Food chains usually overlap to form a food web!' explains mum. 'The highest consumer in the food chain is called the apex predator,' Charlie's mum says, as she licks his face clean with her tongue. 'We're the apex predators at the top of the food chain. Because there are not many of us, there are too many primary and secondary consumers. This leads to overgrazing of the land.'

'We are already experiencing problems with global warming. But this imbalance in the ecosystem is making global warming worse,' she says sadly.

'But Mum, why is this so? Why are there so few cheetahs around?' Charlie asks curiously.

Mum's sad face gets even more sad. It looks like she is going to cry.

'There are fewer and fewer cheetahs around because humans are hunting and killing them,' she replies helplessly. 'As a result, cheetahs have become endangered. But getting rid of cheetahs affects other species as well. It causes a chain reaction that affects our ecosystem!'

'If only humans knew more about keeping the balance in the ecosystem,' Charlie thinks.

Charlie yawns. As he doses off, he dreams of having a better life, with more cheetah cubs to play with. What role could he play in saving the Cheetah from extinction? How could he save this fine balance in our ecosystem?

Facts about Cheetahs

Most of the wild cheetahs left in the world are found in Sub-Saharan Africa, where they roam the grassy and open savannah plains. Cheetahs grow up to 1.3 m in length. They have pale yellow coats with black dots on the upper trunk. Their underbellies are white. Their faces have distinct black lines that curve from the inner corner of each of their eyes to the outer corners of their mouths.

A cheetah can reach speeds of up to 110 km/h in just three seconds which makes it the fastest land animal in the world. Cheetahs are carnivores and live off other animals such as rabbits, warthogs, springboks, gazelles and birds. They hunt during the day. They are apex predators and are at the top of the food chain.

Facts about the effects of human activity on the Cheetah

Cheetahs face extinction pressure from hunting by humans, climate change and habitat destruction due to farming and industrialization, which is reducing the size of their populations. The Cheetah is classified as a threatened species and an estimated 7000 only remain in Africa today.

"As all ecosystems are connected,
helping cheetahs can help the planet as a whole"

Muhammad Wadee encourages the youth to get involved with conservation projects in South Africa and to get involved with initiatives to save planet Earth by reducing, reusing and recycling. All profits from sale of the book will go to Cheetah Rescue Centres in South Africa, as well as to Kids Animal Foundation for the development of water wells in National Parks.

"What humans do over the next 50 years
will determine the fate of all life on the planet."

Sir David Attenborough

"The greatest threat to our planet
is the belief that someone else will save it."

Robert Swan

About the Author

Muhammad Wadee is a budding environmentalist and lives in Johannesburg, South Africa. He is only 11 years old and is amongst South Africa's youngest authors. He lives with his parents Ashraf and Kareema and his siblings Ammaarah, Taskeen and Mahdiyyah Wadee. In his free time, he enjoys reading, doing science experiments and practicing his padel tennis skills which he is most passionate about! He attends St. John's College Preparatory School in Johannesburg where he has learnt accountability and to pursue his dreams. He has been inspired to take on the challenge of writing, with the intention of creating awareness amongst the youth about conservation and the need to make a change.

Printed in the United States
by Baker & Taylor Publisher Services